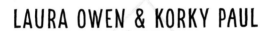

Go, Winnie, Go!

LAURA OWEN & KORKY PAUL

OXFORD

Helping your child to read

Before they start

* Talk about the back cover blurb. Has your child ever seen motor-racing on TV? What might happen when Winnie enters a motor-race on her broomstick?
* Look at the cover picture. Does it give any clue about what might happen in the stories?

During reading

* Let your child read at their own pace, either silently or out loud.
* If necessary, help them to work out words they don't know by saying each sound out loud and then blending them to say a word, e.g. *a-f-t-er-w-ar-d-s, afterwards.*
* Encourage your child to keep checking that the text makes sense and they understand what they are reading. Remind them to reread to check the meaning if they're not sure.
* Give them lots of praise for good reading!

After reading

* Look at page 48 for some fun activities.

Contents

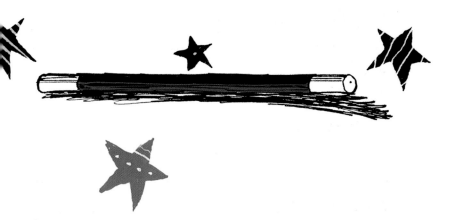

OXFORD
UNIVERSITY PRESS

Great Clarendon Street, Oxford OX2 6DP
Oxford University Press is a department of the University of Oxford.
It furthers the University's objective of excellence in research, scholarship,
and education by publishing worldwide. Oxford is a registered trade mark
of Oxford University Press in the UK and in certain other countries

"Whizz-Bang Winnie" was first published in *Whizz-Bang Winnie* 2010
"Giddy-Up, Winnie" was first published in *Giddy-Up Winnie* 2010
This edition published 2018

The moral rights of the author/illustrator have been asserted

Database right Oxford University Press (maker)

British Library Cataloguing in Publication Data

Data available

ISBN: 978-0-19-276525-3

1 3 5 7 9 10 8 6 4 2

Printed in China

Acknowledgements
With thanks to Catherine Baker for editorial support

Whizz-Bang Winnie

Chapter One

Winnie and Wilbur were flying over the village. "Oooh, look at that!" said Winnie. "Fancy hanging your washing all over the street!"

She zoomed in for a closer look. "Oooh, no! It's not knickers and socks, it's flags and bunting! There must be something special happening today. Let's find out what it is!"

They landed beside a man on a ladder, who was tying up the bunting. **Whoops!** He wobbled when he saw them.

"What's going on?" Winnie asked the man.

"There's a big race this afternoon," said the man.

"What sort of race?" asked Winnie.

"Fast cars with big fat wheels that zoom round corners." The man smiled happily.

8

"It'll be a really exciting race. Lots of noise.
A few crashes. Tea afterwards."

"What sort of noise?" asked Winnie.

"Like this: brrrrrrroooooom!" said
the man.

"Oh, I've got a broom!" said Winnie,
waving her broom at the man.

The man laughed at Winnie. "That's a broom for cleaning, not for racing!" he said. Then he tied the last knot of the bunting string to the lamppost, and climbed down his ladder.

"I could race you on this broom and beat you any day!" said Winnie.

"Meeow!" agreed Wilbur. He swiped his paw past the man's eyes to show him what Winnie's broom could do.

"Well," said the man, "if I were you, I'd keep that broom in the kitchen and leave the racing to the men in the big cars."

"Huh!" said Winnie. "I'll be in that race, just you wait and see!"

The man shook his head. "You can't go in for the race if your vehicle hasn't got wheels." He pointed to a poster.

But Winnie wasn't put off. "There's nothing to stop a broom having wheels, is there?" she said. "Come on, Wilbur! Let's go on a wheel hunt."

11

✦ Chapter ✦ Two

Winnie and Wilbur looked everywhere.

Before long, they found some wheels
of different shapes and sizes in the
bottom of the rubbish bin. They were
a bit odd-looking, though.

"Hand me the hammer, Wilbur," said
Winnie. She took a hammer and began …

bang bang- banging

the wheels onto her broom.

"There, Wilbur, isn't that the best
wheelie broom you've ever seen? Hop on,
you can try it out!"

Poor Wilbur wasn't keen. His knees were knocking together loudly.

"Put on your helmet." Winnie rammed a bucket onto Wilbur's head.

"Hold tight!" said Winnie. Wilbur closed his eyes and hung on tight.

"**Abracadabra!**" shouted Winnie, waving her hand to make the broom go fast. The broom shot forward ... and round in a circle.

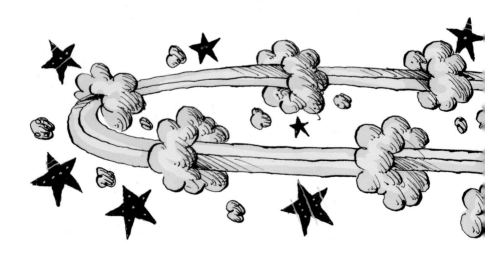

Round and round and round it went, so fast it was just a blur of stick and twigs and frightened cat.

"Oh, bother!" said Winnie. "We'll never win the race like that!"

"Meeeeoooooowwwww!" wailed Wilbur.

"Oh, poor Wilbur!" said Winnie, snatching up her wand. "**Abracadabra!**"

Instantly the broom stopped still. But Wilbur didn't. He shot forward and landed with a crash.

Lurch-skid-clatter-bang! Bang!

"Ouch!"

Winnie fixed the wheels again: this time with bigger wheels at the back and smaller wheels at the front.

"Hop on, Wilbur, and we'll try again," said Winnie.

"Meeow!" Wilbur tried to run, but Winnie plonked him on the broom. "Don't worry, I'm coming with you this time!" she said. "We won't go too fast."

Winnie pulled the broom to the top of the hill. She sat on it, then pushed off ...

whee-hup-bump!

"Stop!" shouted Winnie, but the broom didn't stop. It went faster, and the **hup-bump** got faster, too. "Where's my wand?" screeched Winnie. "**Abra—!**" But Winnie's wand caught in one of the wheels.

17

Lurch-
skid-
clatter-
bang!

"Ouch!"

"Meeowch!"

Winnie and Wilbur were all **bumped**
and **bruised** and **banged** and **biffed**. They
looked at the broken broom.

"We won't win any races on that!"
said Winnie.

★ Chapter ★
Three

Just then, they heard a loudspeaker down in the village announcing the race.

"It's about to start!" said Winnie. "Come on, Wilbur! Even if we can't go in for the race, we can watch it! How can we get there fast? I know … **Abracadabra!**"

In an instant, Winnie had roller skates on her feet.

Crash! She fell over.

"**Ouch!**" said Winnie. "You need some skates too, Wilbur!"

She thought for a moment, then said, "**Abracadabra!**"

Splat! Wilbur instantly had a little wheel under each paw, and those wheels all went in different directions. Out went his legs. Down went Wilbur.

"Meeow!"

"Come on, Wilbur!" cried Winnie.
"We're off!"

Winnie and Wilbur wobbled, then rolled off, getting braver all the time. Soon Winnie was skating along like a champion.

"Wheeeeee! Speeeeedy meeeee!" went Winnie.

There was a sound of engines revving. The cars were off on the race!

Winnie and Wilbur sped off, too.

Soon they got to the hill that ran down to the village. Just then, the cars came around the corner.

"Oooh, Wilbur, this is a bit toooooo faaaaaaast!" shouted Winnie.

Winnie and Wilbur shot onto the road, whizzing past roaring cars. They definitely were going a bit too fast.

"Wiiiilllllbbbbbuuuurrrrr!" shouted
Winnie. "How do I make the skates stop?"

But Wilbur didn't know either.

"Mmmeeeeeeoooooooowwwww!"

Then suddenly Winnie and Wilbur
stopped, tangled up in tape.

"HOORAY!" shouted the crowd.

"Why are they cheering?" said Winnie.
"Look at all my bruises!"

"They're cheering because you won the race, Winnie!" said Jerry, Winnie's giant friend from next door. He had come to watch the race. "Shall I carry you and Wilbur home?"

"That would be lovely," said Winnie. "I'll make us all a nice cup of garlic blossom and ditchwater tea. There's nothing like a proper race, with lots of noise, a few crashes, and tea afterwards."

"Lovely!" said Jerry.

Giddy-Up,
Winnie

26

✯ Chapter ✯
One

Winnie was bouncing up and down on her sofa and whacking the air with her wand. She was excited to be watching the horse-racing on the TV.

"Come on!" she shouted at the screen. "Faster! Go on!"

Then a dreamy look came into Winnie's eyes. "Wouldn't it be wonderful to have our own horse, Wilbur?" she said. "We could go racing!"

"Meeow!" Wilbur shook his head.

Winnie looked at her wand, and then at a rat on the floor. "Wilbur, in Cinderella, they turned a rat into a horse. Let's try it!" she said. Winnie waved her wand. "**Abracadabra!**"

Suddenly there was a horse standing where the rat had been. It was big and cloppy and clumsy. **Crash!** Things fell over as the horse turned around. **Scrunch! Tinkle! Smash!** Winnie's favourite vase went flying.

"Steady, boy!" said Winnie. "Er, you don't look like a racing horse. And that's my hair, not hay, you cloppy great creature! Now, let me think, where's the best place to put you? Let's try the kitchen."

28

Winnie filled the sink with water for the
horse. She fed it carrots and sugar lumps.

Chomp! Chomp!

"Those sugar cubes didn't last long!"
said Winnie.

She put a blanket over the horse. "Go to
sleep now," she said. "We're going racing in
the morning!"

Winnie got into bed, and quickly fell asleep. Soon she was dreaming.

First, Winnie dreamed the Queen was giving her a huge gold cup for winning the race. Then she dreamed she gave the horse a drink of champagne from the cup. The champagne bubbles went up the horse's nose and made him float up into the air, so Winnie grabbed his tail and floated upwards too, and then …

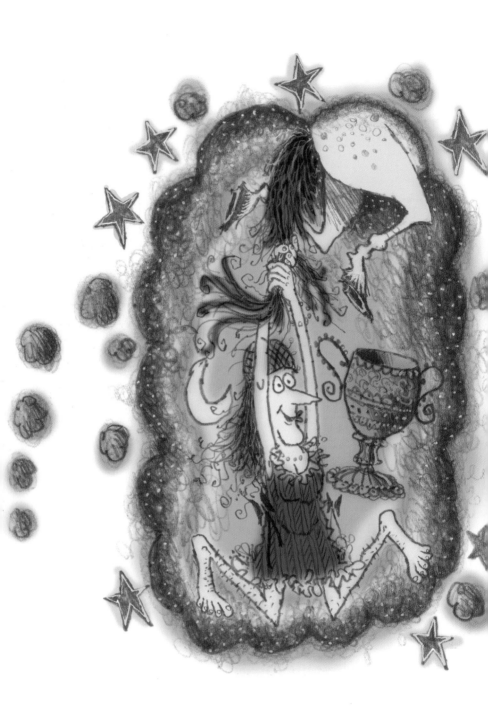

… a horrible pong woke Winnie.

"Stinky!" said Winnie, as she and Wilbur went into the kitchen.

"**Neigh!**" said the horse.

"Meeow!" said Wilbur.

There were piles of steamy horse poo all over the floor.

Winnie grabbed her broom and started to sweep it up. "This isn't the fun bit of having a horse," said Winnie. "But racing will be as fun as an iced cherry bun. Let's get going!"

Chapter Two

Winnie dressed up as a jockey, and put her smallest cauldron on her head as a hat.

"Hey, Wilbur," she said, "we need a proper racing kind of name for our horse. How about Whinny Wonder?"

"Meeow." Wilbur wasn't impressed.

"Well, what about Wilbur and Winnie's Winning Wonder? We can call him Four Ws for short."

"Meeow!" Wilbur thought it was a good idea.

Winnie carefully climbed onto the horse's back. "Oooh! It's very high up!" she called down to Wilbur. "And it's as wide as a whale to sit on!"

Then Winnie clicked her tongue. She was ready to go! "Come on, Four Ws," she said. "Gee-up!"

Nothing happened.

Wilbur looked up nervously. All he could see of Winnie were two legs dangling in the air.

Winnie dangled a sugar lump from the end of her wand. She waved it in front of Four Ws. He stretched his neck to snatch the sugar lump, but he didn't move.

Winnie kicked with her heels. Then she wiggled her bottom. "Get moving, you useless great thing!" she yelled.

Still nothing happened ... until Winnie cracked her broomstick in the air, and Four Ws reared up on his back legs.

WHUMP!

Neigh!

Suddenly, Four Ws was off, galloping
on clip-clopping hooves straight out of
Winnie's house.

"I didn't think he'd be this fast!"
said Winnie.

★ Chapter ★ Three

They didn't get very far. Wilbur fell off
when Four Ws jumped the garden gate.
After a while Winnie fell off, too, and
landed on her cauldron helmet. **Clink!**
Clang! Then she bounced into a ditch full
of smelly, green goo. Slop! Plop!

"Oh, warty toad-toes!" said Winnie,
pulling pond creatures from her hair.

Winnie squelched sadly home. She found
Wilbur busy stuffing mouse nests into one of
Winnie's pongy, holey old socks.

"What are you up to?" asked Winnie,
rubbing her bruises.

Wilbur pulled the sock over the top of Winnie's broomstick, and suddenly Winnie understood what he was doing.

"You're making a hobby-horse!" she said. "Oooh, you clever cat, Wilbur! But it looks more like a hobby-zebra with those stripes!"

Winnie added half boiled-egg eyes and cabbage-leaf ears to her broom hobby-zebra-horse-thing.

"Come on, Wilbur!" she said. "Come on, Broomy! If we're quick we can still be in the last race!"

They hurried to the racetrack, hearing the cheers of the crowd and loudspeaker announcements as they got nearer.

"The last race of the day is the all-comers race," said the announcer. "Horses to the paddock, please."

"Quick! said Winnie to Wilbur
and Broomy.

They got there just in time.

They joined the parade of horses and
jockeys. People pointed and laughed at
Winnie's horse.

"Take no notice, Wilbur," said Winnie.

All the horses lined up for the start of the race. **Bang!** And they were away! Soon, the proper horses were galloping towards the first jump, and Winnie was hobble-running behind. Then she tripped and tumbled.

"Newts' kneecaps!" said Winnie.

"Ha ha!" laughed the crowd.

"**Abracadabra!**" shouted Winnie.

Winnie's broomstick hobby-zebra-horsey suddenly zoomed after the galloping horses. He swooped easily over the fence. The broomstick hobby-zebra-horsey turned and grinned his awful grin at the horses coming up behind, and half of them ran off in the wrong direction.

"Giddy-up!" said Winnie, and Broomy whizzed forwards. Then he suddenly screeched to a halt. The other riders tried to stop, too, and crashed into one another.

Thump! Bump!

"There's only one horse in front of us now!" shouted Winnie. "Come on, Broomy! I'll never use you for sweeping horse poo again if you win the race!"

Broomy went faster and faster … and he won the race by a cabbage ear.

"Hooray!" shouted Winnie.

"Hooray!" shouted the crowd.

"You can't have the winning cup," said a snooty man in a hat. "That's only for riders of real horses."

"I don't mind," said Winnie. "I've got my own prize." She took something from her pocket, popped it into her mouth and began to crunch. She patted Broomy on the nose. "That's the best thing about a hobby horse," she said with a grin. "You can eat the sugar lumps yourself!"

After reading activities

Quick quiz

See how fast you can answer these questions! Look back at the stories if you can't remember.

1. In "Whizz-Bang Winnie", how does Wilbur feel about going on the wheelie-broom?

2. In "Whizz-Bang Winnie", what kind of wheels are Winnie and Wilbur using when they win the race?

3. In "Giddy-Up, Winnie", what is Winnie's horse called?

1. he's scared. 2. roller skates. 3. Wilbur and Winnie's Winning Wonder, or Four Ws for short.

Talk about it!

★ In "Whizz-Bang Winnie", why do you think Winnie doesn't realise she's won the race?

★ In "Giddy-Up, Winnie", do you think it's fair that the judge won't let Winnie have the winning cup? Why, or why not?